THE COMEDY OF ERRORS

DOVER THRIFT EDITIONS

William Shakespeare

DOVER PUBLICATIONS, INC.
MINEOLA, NEW YORK

DOVER THRIFT EDITIONS

GENERAL EDITOR: PAUL NEGRI
EDITOR OF THIS VOLUME: SUSAN L. RATTINER

Copyright

Theatrical Rights

Bibliographical Note

This Dover edition, first published in 2002, contains the unabridged text of *The Comedy of Errors* as published in Volume I of *The Caxton Edition of the Complete Works of William Shakespeare*, Caxton Publishing Company, London, n.d. The Note was prepared specially for this edition.

Library of Congress Cataloging-in-Publication Data

Shakespeare, William, 1564–1616.
    The comedy of errors / William Shakespeare.
        p. cm. — (Dover thrift editions)
    ISBN-13: 978-0-486-42461-3 (pbk.)
    ISBN-10: 0-486-42461-8 (pbk.)
    1. Survival after airplane accidents, shipwrecks, etc.—Drama. 2. Mistaken identity—Drama. 3. Brothers—Drama. 4. Greece—Drama. 5. Twins—Drama. I. Title. II. Series.

PR2804 .A1 2002
822.3'3—dc21

2002024485

Manufactured in the United States by LSC Communications
42461811   2020
www.doverpublications.com

Note

WILLIAM SHAKESPEARE (1564–1616) was born in Stratford-on-Avon, Warwickshire, England. Although much of his early life remains sketchy, it is known that he moved to London ca. 1589 to earn his way as an actor and playwright. He joined an acting company known as the Lord Chamberlain's Men in 1594, a decision that finally enabled him to share in the financial success of his plays. Only eighteen of his thirty-seven plays were published during his lifetime, and these were usually sold directly to theater companies and printed in quartos, or single-play editions, without his approval.

The Comedy of Errors, one of Shakespeare's earliest and shortest plays, is primarily based on *Menæchmi* by the Roman playwright Plautus. Plautus' work follows the misadventures of a set of twin brothers with the same name who were separated at birth. Shakespeare's version of the work far outshines the original in comic suspense and surprise after he added another set of twins—the brothers' servants—to the mix. Only when the two pairs of twins career through multiple misunderstandings does the mastery of Shakespeare's comedic construction become clear.

Contents

Dramatis Personæ[1]

SOLINUS, duke of Ephesus.
ÆGEON, a merchant of Syracuse.
ANTIPHOLUS of Ephesus, ⎤ twin brothers, and sons to
ANTIPHOLUS of Syracuse, ⎦ Ægeon and Æmilia.
DROMIO of Ephesus, ⎤ twin brothers, and attendants on
DROMIO of Syracuse, ⎦ the two Antipholuses.
BALTHAZAR, a merchant.
ANGELO, a goldsmith.
First Merchant, friend to Antipholus of Syracuse.
Second Merchant, to whom Angelo is a debtor.
PINCH, a schoolmaster.

ÆMILIA, wife to Ægeon, an abbess at Ephesus.
ADRIANA, wife to Antipholus of Ephesus.
LUCIANA, her sister.
LUCE, servant to Adriana.
A Courtezan.

Gaoler, Officers, and other Attendants.
SCENE—*Ephesus*

[1]This play was first printed in the First Folio. The *Dramatis Personæ* was first supplied in Nicholas Rowe's edition of 1709.

ACT I.

SCENE I. A *Hall in the Duke's Palace.*

Enter DUKE, ÆGEON, Gaoler, Officers, *and other* Attendants

ÆGEON.   Proceed, Solinus, to procure my fall,
  And by the doom of death end woes and all.
DUKE.   Merchant of Syracusa, plead no more;
  I am not partial to infringe our laws:
  The enmity and discord which of late
  Sprung from the rancorous outrage of your duke
  To merchants, our well-dealing countrymen,
  Who, wanting guilders to redeem their lives,
  Have seal'd his rigorous statutes with their bloods,
  Excludes all pity from our threatening looks.   10
  For, since the mortal and intestine jars
  'Twixt thy seditious countrymen and us,
  It hath in solemn synods been decreed,
  Both by the Syracusians and ourselves,
  To admit no traffic to our adverse towns:
  Nay, more,
  If any born at Ephesus be seen
  At any Syracusian marts and fairs;
  Again: if any Syracusian born
  Come to the bay of Ephesus, he dies,   20
  His goods confiscate to the duke's dispose;
  Unless a thousand marks be levied,
  To quit the penalty and to ransom him.
  Thy substance, valued at the highest rate,
  Cannot amount unto a hundred marks;
  Therefore by law thou art condemn'd to die.

4 *partial*] inclined.
8 *guilders*] money. Cf. IV, i, 4, *infra*. The word reproduces the Dutch "gulden," a stan-
  dard coin of the Low Countries, a silver piece worth about 40 cents, or 1*s*. 8*d*.

1

ÆGE.   Yet this my comfort: when your words are done,
        My woes end likewise with the evening sun.
DUKE.   Well, Syracusian, say, in brief, the cause
        Why thou departed'st from thy native home,   30
        And for what cause thou camest to Ephesus.
ÆGE.   A heavier task could not have been imposed
        Than I to speak my griefs unspeakable:
        Yet, that the world may witness that my end
        Was wrought by nature, not by vile offence,
        I'll utter what my sorrow gives me leave.
        In Syracusa was I born; and wed
        Unto a woman, happy but for me,
        And by me, had not our hap been bad.
        With her I lived in joy; our wealth increased   40
        By prosperous voyages I often made
        To Epidamnum; till my factor's death,
        And the great care of goods at random left,
        Drew me from kind embracements of my spouse:
        From whom my absence was not six months old,
        Before herself, almost at fainting under
        The pleasing punishment that women bear,
        Had made provision for her following me,
        And soon and safe arrived where I was.
        There had she not been long but she became   50
        A joyful mother of two goodly sons;
        And, which was strange, the one so like the other
        As could not be distinguish'd but by names.
        That very hour, and in the self-same inn,
        A meaner woman was delivered
        Of such a burthen, male twins, both alike:
        Those, for their parents were exceeding poor,
        I bought, and brought up to attend my sons.
        My wife, not meanly proud of two such boys,
        Made daily motions for our home return: 60
        Unwilling I agreed; alas! too soon
        We came aboard.
        A league from Epidamnum had we sail'd,
        Before the always-wind-obeying deep
        Gave any tragic instance of our harm:

---

35 *nature*] natural affection.
42 *Epidamnum*] The Folio reading is *Epidamium. Epidamnum*, which is Pope's correction, has been generally adopted. It is the form found in W. W.'s translation of Plautus' *Menæchmi*, 1595. The correct name of the town is "Epidamnos."

But longer did we not retain much hope;
For what obscured light the heavens did grant
Did but convey unto our fearful minds
A doubtful warrant of immediate death;
Which though myself would gladly have embraced,   70
Yet the incessant weepings of my wife,
Weeping before for what she saw must come,
And piteous plainings of the pretty babes,
That mourn'd for fashion, ignorant what to fear,
Forced me to seek delays for them and me.
And this it was, for other means was none:
The sailors sought for safety by our boat,
And left the ship, then sinking-ripe, to us:
My wife, more careful for the latter-born,
Had fasten'd him unto a small spare mast,   80
Such as seafaring men provide for storms;
To him one of the other twins was bound,
Whilst I had been like heedful of the other:
The children thus disposed, my wife and I,
Fixing our eyes on whom our care was fix'd,
Fasten'd ourselves at either end the mast;
And floating straight, obedient to the stream,
Was carried towards Corinth, as we thought.
At length the sun, gazing upon the earth,
Dispersed those vapours that offended us;   90
And, by the benefit of his wished light,
The seas wax'd calm, and we discovered
Two ships from far making amain to us,
Of Corinth that, of Epidaurus this:
But ere they came,—O, let me say no more!
Gather the sequel by that went before.
DUKE.   Nay, forward, old man; do not break off so;
For we may pity, though not pardon thee.
ÆGE.   O, had the gods done so, I had not now
Worthily term'd them merciless to us!   100
For, ere the ships could meet by twice five leagues,
We were encounter'd by a mighty rock;
Which being violently borne upon,
Our helpful ship was splitted in the midst;
So that, in this unjust divorce of us,
Fortune had left to both of us alike
What to delight in, what to sorrow for.
Her part, poor soul! seeming as burdened

With lesser weight, but not with lesser woe,
Was carried with more speed before the wind; 110
And in our sight they three were taken up
By fishermen of Corinth, as we thought.
At length, another ship had seized on us;
And, knowing whom it was their hap to save,
Gave healthful welcome to their shipwreck'd guests;
And would have reft the fishers of their prey,
Had not their bark been very slow of sail;
And therefore homeward did they bend their course.
Thus have you heard me sever'd from my bliss;
That by misfortunes was my life prolong'd, 120
To tell sad stories of my own mishaps.

DUKE. And for the sake of them thou sorrowest for,
Do me the favour to dilate at full
What hath befall'n of them and thee till now.

ÆGE. My youngest boy, and yet my eldest care,
At eighteen years became inquisitive
After his brother: and importuned me
That his attendant—so his case was like,
Reft of his brother, but retain'd his name—
Might bear him company in the quest of him: 130
Whom whilst I labour'd of a love to see,
I hazarded the loss of whom I loved.
Five summers have I spent in farthest Greece,
Roaming clean through the bounds of Asia,
And, coasting homeward, came to Ephesus;
Hopeless to find, yet loath to leave unsought
Or that, or any place that harbours men.
But here must end the story of my life;
And happy were I in my timely death,
Could all my travels warrant me they live. 140

DUKE. Hapless Ægeon, whom the fates have mark'd
To bear the extremity of dire mishap!
Now, trust me, were it not against our laws,
Against my crown, my oath, my dignity,
Which princes, would they, may not disannul,
My soul should sue as advocate for thee.

---

125 *My youngest boy, etc.*] This does not quite harmonise with other passages of
Ægeon's story; at lines 79 and 110 he describes himself as separated from his "latter-
born" son, who is carried away from him along with his wife. The discrepancy is
due to Shakespeare's hasty composition.

131 *labour'd of a love*] was troubled by a desire.

But, though thou art adjudged to the death,
And passed sentence may not be recall'd
But to our honour's great disparagement,
Yet will I favour thee in what I can.   150
Therefore, merchant, I'll limit thee this day
To seek thy help by beneficial help:
Try all the friends thou hast in Ephesus;
Beg thou, or borrow, to make up the sum,
And live; if no, then thou art doom'd to die.
Gaoler, take him to thy custody.

GAOL.   I will, my lord.

ÆGE.   Hopeless and helpless doth Ægeon wend,
But to procrastinate his lifeless end.

                                                    [*Exeunt.*

SCENE II. *The Mart.*

Enter ANTIPHOLUS of Syracuse, DROMIO of Syracuse, *and* First
    Merchant

FIRST MER.   Therefore give out you are of Epidamnum,
Lest that your goods too soon be confiscate.
This very day a Syracusian merchant
Is apprehended for arrival here;
And, not being able to buy out his life,
According to the statute of the town,
Dies ere the weary sun set in the west
There is your money that I had to keep.

ANT. S.   Go bear it to the Centaur, where we host,
And stay there, Dromio, till I come to thee.   10
Within this hour it will be dinner-time:
Till that, I'll view the manners of the town,
Peruse the traders, gaze upon the buildings,
And then return, and sleep within mine inn;
For with long travel I am stiff and weary.
Get thee away.

DRO. S.   Many a man would take you at your word,
And go indeed, having so good a mean.

                                                    [*Exit.*

ANT. S.   A trusty villain, sir; that very oft,
When I am dull with care and melancholy,   20
Lightens my humour with his merry jests.
What, will you walk with me about the town,

And then go to my inn, and dine with me?

FIRST MER.   I am invited, sir, to certain merchants,
Of whom I hope to make much benefit;
I crave your pardon. Soon at five o'clock,
Please you, I'll meet with you upon the mart,
And afterward consort you till bed-time:
My present business calls me from you now.   ·

ANT. S.   Farewell till then: I will go lose myself,   30
And wander up and down to view the city.

FIRST MER.   Sir, I commend you to your own content.

[*Exit.*

ANT. S.   He that commends me to mine own content
Commends me to the thing I cannot get.
I to the world am like a drop of water,
That in the ocean seeks another drop;
Who, falling there to find his fellow forth,
Unseen, inquisitive, confounds himself:
So I, to find a mother and a brother,
In quest of them, unhappy, lose myself.   40

Enter DROMIO of Ephesus

Here comes the almanac of my true date.
What now? how chance thou art return'd so soon?

DRO. E.   Return'd so soon! rather approach'd too late:
The capon burns, the pig falls from the spit;
The clock hath strucken twelve upon the bell;
My mistress made it one upon my cheek:
She is so hot, because the meat is cold;
The meat is cold, because you come not home;
You come not home, because you have no stomach;
You have no stomach, having broke your fast;   50
But we, that know what 't is to fast and pray,
Are penitent for your default to-day.

ANT. S.   Stop in your wind, sir: tell me this, I pray:
Where have you left the money that I gave you?

DRO. E.   O,—sixpence, that I had o' Wednesday last
To pay the saddler for my mistress' crupper?

---

28 *consort you*] accompany you. Cf. *L. L. L.,* II, i, 177: "Sweet health and fair desires *consort* your Grace"; *Rom. & Jul.,* III, i, 135, and *Jul. Caes.,* V, i, 83.

38 *confounds*] destroys, loses.

41 *almanac . . . date*] The speaker was born at the same hour as the newcomer, who is therefore called the indicator of the other's true date of birth.

52 *Are penitent*] Suffer penance (by fasting and praying).

The saddler had it, sir; I kept it not.

ANT. S.   I am not in a sportive humour now:
Tell me, and dally not, where is the money?
We being strangers here, how darest thou trust   60
So great a charge from thine own custody?

DRO. E.   I pray you, jest, sir, as you sit at dinner:
I from my mistress come to you in post;
If I return, I shall be post indeed,
For she will score your fault upon my pate.
Methinks your maw, like mine, should be your clock,
And strike you home without a messenger.

ANT. S.   Come, Dromio, come, these jests are out of season;
Reserve them till a merrier hour than this.
Where is the gold I gave in charge to thee?   70

DRO. E.   To me, sir? why, you gave no gold to me.

ANT. S.   Come on, sir knave, have done your foolishness,
And tell me how thou hast disposed thy charge.

DRO. E.   My charge was but to fetch you from the mart
Home to your house, the Phœnix, sir, to dinner:
My mistress and her sister stays for you.

ANT. S.   Now, as I am a Christian, answer me,
In what safe place you have bestow'd my money;
Or I shall break that merry sconce of yours,
That stands on tricks when I am undisposed: 80
Where is the thousand marks thou had'st of me?

DRO. E.   I have some marks of yours upon my pate,
Some of my mistress' marks upon my shoulders;
But not a thousand marks between you both.
If I should pay your worship those again,
Perchance you will not bear them patiently.

ANT. S.   Thy mistress' marks? what mistress, slave, hast thou?

DRO. E.   Your worship's wife, my mistress at the Phœnix;
She that doth fast till you come home to dinner,
And prays that you will hie you home to dinner.   90

ANT. S.   What, wilt thou flout me thus unto my face,
Being forbid? There, take you that, sir knave.

63–65 *post . . . score*] A post usually stood in the middle of a shop or a tavern, and on it
the scores of customers were chalked up. The words in line 63, *in post*, which sug-
gest the quibble, mean "in haste."
66 *clock*] Pope's emendation of the original reading *cook*.
80 *stands on tricks*] indulges in tricks.

DRO. E.   What mean you, sir? for God's sake, hold your hands!
    Nay, an you will not, sir, I'll take my heels.

                                                    [*Exit.*

ANT. S.   Upon my life, by some device or other
    The villain is o'er-raught of all my money.
    They say this town is full of cozenage;
    As, nimble jugglers that deceive the eye,
    Dark-working sorcerers that change the mind,
    Soul-killing witches that deform the body,   100
    Disguised cheaters, prating mountebanks,
    And many such-like liberties of sin:
    If it prove so, I will be gone the sooner.
    I'll to the Centaur, to go seek this slave
    I greatly fear my money is not safe.

                                                    [*Exit.*

---

96 *o'er-raught*] over-reached, cheated out of, cheated.
102 *liberties of sin*] Hanmer reads *libertines.* Steevens explains "licensed offenders."
    Malone gives the more probable interpretation, "licentious actions."

ACT II.

SCENE I. *The House of Antipholus of Ephesus.*

Enter ADRIANA *and* LUCIANA

ADRIANA. Neither my husband nor the slave return'd,
  That in such haste I sent to seek his master!
  Sure, Luciana, it is two o'clock.
LUC. Perhaps some merchant hath invited him,
  And from the mart he's somewhere gone to dinner.
  Good sister, let us dine, and never fret:
  A man is master of his liberty:
  Time is their master; and when they see time,
  They'll go or come: if so, be patient, sister.
ADR. Why should their liberty than ours be more?   10
LUC. Because their business still lies out o' door.
ADR. Look, when I serve him so, he takes it ill.
LUC. O, know he is the bridle of your will.
ADR. There's none but asses will be bridled so.
LUC. Why, headstrong liberty is lash'd with woe.
  There's nothing situate under heaven's eye
  But hath his bound, in earth, in sea, in sky:
  The beasts, the fishes, and the winged fowls,
  Are their males' subjects and at their controls:
  Men more divine, the masters of all these,   20
  Lords of the wide world and wild watery seas,
  Indued with intellectual sense and souls,
  Of more pre-eminence than fish and fowls,
  Are masters to their females, and their lords:
  Then let your will attend on their accords.
ADR. This servitude makes you to keep unwed.
LUC. Not this, but troubles of the marriage-bed.
ADR. But, were you wedded, you would bear some sway.
LUC. Ere I learn love, I'll practise to obey.

9

ADR. How if your husband start some other where? 30
LUC. Till he come home again, I would forbear.
ADR. Patience unmoved! no marvel though she pause;
    They can be meek that have no other cause.
    A wretched soul, bruised with adversity,
    We bid be quiet when we hear it cry;
    But were we burden'd with like weight of pain,
    As much, or more, we should ourselves complain:
    So thou, that hast no unkind mate to grieve thee,
    With urging helpless patience wouldst relieve me;
    But, if thou live to see like right bereft, 40
    This fool-begg'd patience in thee will be left.
LUC. Well, I will marry one day, but to try.
    Here comes your man; now is your husband nigh.

Enter DROMIO of Ephesus

ADR. Say, is your tardy master now at hand?
DRO. E. Nay, he's at two hands with me, and that my two ears
    can witness.
ADR. Say, didst thou speak with him? know'st thou his mind?
DRO. E. Ay, ay, he told his mind upon mine ear:
    Beshrew his hand, I scarce could understand it.
LUC. Spake he so doubtfully, thou couldst not feel his meaning? 50
DRO. E. Nay, he struck so plainly, I could too well feel his blows;
    and withal so doubtfully, that I could scarce understand
    them.
ADR. But say, I prithee, is he coming home?
    It seems he hath great care to please his wife.
DRO. E. Why, mistress, sure my master is horn-mad.
ADR. Horn-mad, thou villain!
DRO. E.   I mean not cuckold-mad;
    But, sure, he is stark mad.
    When I desired him to come home to dinner, 60
    He ask'd me for a thousand marks in gold:
    "'T is dinner-time," quoth I; "My gold!" quoth he:
    "Your meat doth burn," quoth I; "My gold!" quoth he:
    "Will you come home?" quoth I; "My gold!" quoth he,
    "Where is the thousand marks I gave thee, villain?"
    "The pig," quoth I, "is burn'd;" "My gold!" quoth he:

41 *fool-begg'd*] admittedly or notoriously foolish. There is an allusion to the custom of
    begging or petitioning for the guardianship of any one who was admitted to be a fool.
    Here patience is personified as the "fool" whose guardianship is begged.
52 *understand*] stand under: a poor quibble.

   "My mistress, sir," quoth I; "Hang up thy mistress!
   I know not thy mistress; out on thy mistress!"
LUC.   Quoth who?
DRO. E.   Quoth my master: 70
   "I know," quoth he, "no house, no wife, no mistress."
   So that my errand, due unto my tongue,
   I thank him, I bare home upon my shoulders;
   For, in conclusion, he did beat me there.
ADR.   Go back again, thou slave, and fetch him home.
DRO. E.   Go back again, and be new beaten home?
   For God's sake, send some other messenger.
ADR.   Back, slave, or I will break thy pate across.
DRO. E.   And he will bless that cross with other beating:
   Between you I shall have a holy head.   80
ADR.   Hence, prating peasant! fetch thy master home.
DRO. E.   Am I so round with you as you with me,
   That like a football you do spurn me thus?
   You spurn me hence, and he will spurn me hither:
   If I last in this service, you must case me in leather.
                                      [Exit.

LUC.   Fie, how impatience loureth in your face!
ADR.   His company must do his minions grace,
   Whilst I at home starve for a merry look.
   Hath homely age the alluring beauty took
   From my poor cheek? then he hath wasted it;   90
   Are my discourses dull? barren my wit?
   If voluble and sharp discourse be marr'd,
   Unkindness blunts it more than marble hard:
   Do their gay vestments his affections bait?
   That's not my fault; he's master of my state:
   What ruins are in me that can be found,
   By him not ruin'd? then is he the ground
   Of my defeatures. My decayed fair
   A sunny look of his would soon repair:
   But, too unruly deer, he breaks the pale,   100
   And feeds from home; poor I am but his stale.

---

80 *holy head*] The quibble on *cross* suggests the punning use of *holy* in the sense of "full of holes."

82 *round*] blunt, outspoken. The word quibblingly suggests *football* and *leather* in 83 and 85.

98 *defeatures*] disfigurements. Shakespeare is the only Elizabethan writer who uses the word in this sense, in V, i, 301, *infra*.
   fair] beauty. This substantival use of the adjective is common in Shakespeare's *Sonnets*. Cf. *Sonnets*, xvi, 11; xviii, 7 and 10; lxviii, 3; and lxxxiii, 2.

LUC.   Self-harming jealousy! fie, beat it hence!
ADR.   Unfeeling fools can with such wrongs dispense.
    I know his eye doth homage otherwhere;
    Or else what lets it but he would be here?
    Sister, you know he promised me a chain;
    Would that alone, alone he would detain,
    So he would keep fair quarter with his bed!
    I see the jewel best enamelled
    Will lose his beauty; yet the gold bides still,   110
    That others touch, and often touching will
    Wear gold: and no man that hath a name,
    By falsehood and corruption doth it shame.
    Since that my beauty cannot please his eye,
    I'll weep what's left away, and weeping die.
LUC.   How many fond fools serve mad jealousy!

                                      [*Exeunt.*

SCENE II. *A Public Place.*

Enter ANTIPHOLUS of Syracuse

ANT. S.   The gold I gave to Dromio is laid up
    Safe at the Centaur; and the heedful slave
    Is wander'd forth, in care to seek me out
    By computation and mine host's report.
    I could not speak with Dromio since at first
    I sent him from the mart. See, here he comes.

Enter DROMIO of Syracuse

    How now, sir! is your merry humour alter'd?
    As you love strokes, so jest with me again.
    You know no Centaur? you received no gold?
    Your mistress sent to have me home to dinner?   10
    My house was at the Phœnix? Wast thou mad,
    That thus so madly thou didst answer me?
DRO. S.   What answer, sir? when spake I, such a word?

---

107 *alone, alone*] Thus the Second Folio, which substitutes the second *alone* for the two
    words *a loue* of the First Folio. Though some emendation of the original text is es-
    sential, it is doubtful if the Second Folio reading be correct. Hanmer read *alone, alas.*
110–112 *yet the gold . . . gold*] Thus in the First Folio, save for Theobald's correction of
    Wear for *Where* (l. 112). The meaning seems to be that gold which is touched or
    tested lasts long, and at the same time much touching or handling wears gold down.
113 *By falsehood*] Theobald's reading, *But falsehood*, makes better sense.

ANT. S.   Even now, even here, not half an hour since.

DRO. S.   I did not see you since you sent me hence,
Home to the Centaur, with the gold you gave me.

ANT. S.   Villain, thou didst deny the gold's receipt,
And told'st me of a mistress and a dinner;
For which, I hope, thou felt'st I was displeased.

DRO. S.   I am glad to see you in this merry vein: 20
What means this jest? I pray you, master, tell me.

ANT. S.   Yea, dost thou jeer and flout me in the teeth?
Think'st thou I jest? Hold, take thou that, and that.

[Beating him.

DRO. S.   Hold, sir, for God's sake! now your jest is earnest:
Upon what bargain do you give it me?

ANT. S.   Because that I familiarly sometimes
Do use you for my fool, and chat with you,
Your sauciness will jest upon my love,
And make a common of my serious hours.
When the sun shines let foolish gnats make sport,   30
But creep in crannies when he hides his beams.
If you will jest with me, know my aspect,
And fashion your demeanour to my looks,
Or I will beat this method in your sconce.

DRO. S.   Sconce call you it? so you would leave battering, I had
rather have it a head: an you use these blows long, I must get
a sconce for my head, and insconce it too; or else I shall seek
my wit in my shoulders. But, I pray, sir, why am I beaten?

ANT. S.   Dost thou not know?

DRO. S.   Nothing, sir, but that I am beaten.   40

ANT. S.   Shall I tell you why?

DRO. S.   Ay, sir, and wherefore; for they say every why hath a
wherefore.

ANT. S.   Why, first,—for flouting me; and then, wherefore,—
For urging it the second time to me.

DRO. S.   Was there ever any man thus beaten out of season,
When in the why and the wherefore is neither rhyme nor
reason?
Well, sir, I thank you.

ANT. S.   Thank me, sir! for what?

---

29 *make a common of*] make ground open to all, intrude upon.

34–37 *sconce . . . insconce*] *Sconce* is used at first for "head" and then for "head cover-
ing," or "helmet." Cf. I, ii, 79, *supra*.

37–38 *seek . . . shoulders*] find my wit in my back, *i.e.* run away.

DRO. S. Marry, sir, for this something that you gave me for   50
nothing.

ANT. S. I'll make you amends next, to give you nothing for
something. But say, sir, is it dinner-time?

DRO. S. No, sir: I think the meat wants that I have.

ANT. S. In good time, sir; what's that?

DRO. S. Basting.

ANT. S. Well, sir, then 't will be dry.

DRO. S. If it be, sir, I pray you, eat none of it.

ANT. S. Your reason?

DRO. S. Lest it make you choleric, and purchase me another   60
dry basting.

ANT. S. Well, sir, learn to jest in good time: there's a time for all
things.

DRO. S. I durst have denied that, before you were so choleric.

ANT. S. By what rule, sir?

DRO. S. Marry, sir, by a rule as plain as the plain bald pate of father Time himself.

ANT. S. Let's hear it.

DRO. S. There's no time for a man to recover his hair that grows
bald by nature.   70

ANT. S. May he not do it by fine and recovery?

DRO. S. Yes, to pay a fine for a periwig, and recover the lost hair
of another man.

ANT. S. Why is Time such a niggard of hair, being, as it is, so
plentiful an excrement?

DRO. S. Because it is a blessing that he bestows on beasts: and
what he hath scanted men in hair, he hath given them in
wit.

ANT. S. Why, but there's many a man hath more hair than wit.

DRO. S. Not a man of those but he hath the wit to lose his hair.   80

ANT. S. Why, thou didst conclude hairy men plain dealers without wit.

DRO. S. The plainer dealer, the sooner lost: yet he loseth it in a
kind of jollity.

ANT. S. For what reason?

DRO. S. For two; and sound ones too.

---

60 *choleric*] Cf. *T. of Shrew*, IV, i, 173–175, for a like reference to the choleric effects of
overcooked meat.

61 *dry basting*] beating that does not draw blood.

71 *fine and recovery*] This phrase is employed again in *M. Wives*, IV, ii, 225, and
Hamlet, V, i, 115. It is somewhat loosely employed. "Fine" and "recovery" were
names of legal processes which rendered ownership absolute and incontestable.

80 *lose his hair*] A symptom of venereal disease. Cf. lines 83–84.

ANT. S.   Nay, not sound, I pray you.
DRO. S.   Sure ones, then.
ANT. S.   Nay, not sure, in a thing falsing.
DRO. S.   Certain ones, then.   90
ANT. S.   Name them.
DRO. S.   The one, to save the money that he spends in tiring;
    the other, that at dinner they should not drop in his porridge.
ANT. S.   You would all this time have proved there is no time for
    all things.
DRO. S.   Marry, and did, sir; namely, no time to recover hair lost
    by nature.
ANT. S.   But your reason was not substantial, why there is no
    time to recover.
DRO. S.   Thus I mend it: Time himself is bald, and therefore to   100
    the world's end will have bald followers.
ANT. S.   I knew 't would be a bald conclusion:
    But, soft! who wafts us yonder?

Enter ADRIANA *and* LUCIANA

ADR.   Ay, ay, Antipholus, look strange and frown:
    Some other mistress hath thy sweet aspects;
    I am not Adriana nor thy wife.
    The time was once when thou unurged wouldst vow
    That never words were music to thine ear,
    That never object pleasing in thine eye,
    That never touch well welcome to thy hand,   110
    That never meat sweet-savour'd in thy taste,
    Unless I spake, or look'd, or touch'd, or carved to thee.
    How comes it now, my husband, O, how comes it,
    That thou art then estranged from thyself?
    Thyself I call it, being strange to me,
    That, undividable, incorporate,
    Am better than thy dear self's better part.
    Ah, do not tear away thyself from me!
    For know, my love, as easy mayst thou fall
    A drop of water in the breaking gulf,   120
    And take unmingled thence that drop again,
    Without addition or diminishing,
    As take from me thyself, and not me too.
    How dearly would it touch thee to the quick,

92 *tiring*] dressing. Pope's emendation of the old reading *trying*.
117 *better part*] The soul, as in *Sonnets*, xxxix, 2, lxxiv, 8: "My spirit is thine, the better
    part of me."

Shouldst thou but hear I were licentious,
And that this body consecrate to thee,
By ruffian lust should be contaminate!
Wouldst thou not spit at me and spurn at me,
And hurl the name of husband in my face,
And tear the stain'd skin off my harlot-brow,   130
And from my false hand cut the wedding-ring,
And break it with a deep-divorcing vow?
I know thou canst; and therefore see thou do it.
I am possess'd with an adulterate blot;
My blood is mingled with the crime of lust:
For if we two be one, and thou play false,
I do digest the poison of thy flesh,
Being strumpeted by thy contagion.
Keep, then, fair league and truce with thy true bed;
I live distain'd, thou undishonoured.   140

ANT. S.   Plead you to me, fair dame? I know you not:
In Ephesus I am but two hours old,
As strange unto your town as to your talk;
Who, every word by all my wit being scann'd,
Wants wit in all one word to understand.

LUC.   Fie, brother! how the world is changed with you!
When were you wont to use my sister thus?
She sent for you by Dromio home to dinner.

ANT. S.   By Dromio?

DRO. S.   By me?   150

ADR.   By thee; and this thou didst return from him,
That he did buffet thee, and, in his blows,
Denied my house for his, me for his wife.

ANT. S.   Did you converse, sir, with this gentlewoman?
What is the course and drift of your compact?

DRO. S.   I, sir? I never saw her till this time.

ANT. S.   Villain, thou liest; for even her very words
Didst thou deliver to me on the mart.

DRO. S.   I never spake with her in all my life.

ANT. S.   How can she thus then call us by our names?   160
Unless it be by inspiration.

ADR.   How ill agrees it with your gravity
To counterfeit thus grossly with your slave,
Abetting him to thwart me in my mood!
Be it my wrong you are from me exempt,

---

140 *distain'd*] The sense requires that this word should have the unusual meaning of
"unstained." It ordinarily means "deeply stained," "defiled."

But wrong not that wrong with a more contempt.
Come, I will fasten on this sleeve of thine:
Thou art an elm, my husband, I a vine,
Whose weakness, married to thy stronger state,
Makes me with thy strength to communicate: 170
If aught possess thee from me, it is dross,
Usurping ivy, brier, or idle moss;
Who, all for want of pruning, with intrusion
Infect thy sap, and live on thy confusion.

ANT. S.   To me she speaks; she moves me for her theme:
What, was I married to her in my dream?
Or sleep I now, and think I hear all this?
What error drives our eyes and ears amiss?
Until I know this sure uncertainty,
I'll entertain the offer'd fallacy.   180

LUC.   Dromio, go bid the servants spread for dinner.

DRO. S.   O, for my beads! I cross me for a sinner.
This is the fairy land: O spite of spites!
We talk with goblins, owls, and sprites:
If we obey them not, this will ensue,
They'll suck our breath, or pinch us black and blue.

LUC.   Why pratest thou to thyself, and answer'st not?
Dromio, thou drone, thou snail, thou slug, thou sot!

DRO. S.   I am transformed, master, am not I?

ANT. S.   I think thou art in mind, and so am I.   190

DRO. S.   Nay, master, both in mind and in my shape.

ANT. S.   Thou hast thine own form.

DRO. S.   No, I am an ape.

LUC.   If thou art changed to aught, 't is to an ass.

DRO. S.   'T is true; she rides me, and I long for grass.
'T is so, I am an ass; else it could never be
But I should know her as well as she knows me.

ADR.   Come, come, no longer will I be a fool,
To put the finger in the eye and weep,
Whilst man and master laughs my woes to scorn.   200
Come, sir, to dinner. Dromio, keep the gate.
Husband, I'll dine above with you to-day,
And shrive you of a thousand idle pranks.
Sirrah, if any ask you for your master,
Say he dines forth, and let no creature enter.
Come, sister. Dromio, play the porter well.

---

184 *sprites*] Pope completed the line by inserting *elvish* before *sprites*; the change has
   been generally adopted.

ANT. S.   Am I in earth, in heaven, or in hell?
    Sleeping or waking? mad or well-advised?
    Known unto these, and to myself disguised!
    I'll say as they say, and persever so,   210
    And in this midst at all adventures go.
DRO. S.   Master, shall I be porter at the gate?
ADR.   Ay; and let none enter, lest I break your pate.
LUC.   Come, come, Antipholus, we dine too late.

                                  [Exeunt.

ACT III.

SCENE I. *Before the House of Antipholus of Ephesus.*

Enter ANTIPHOLUS *of* Ephesus, DROMIO *of* Ephesus, ANGELO,
and BALTHAZAR

ANTIPHOLUS E.   Good Signior Angelo, you must excuse us all;
My wife is shrewish when I keep not hours:
Say that I linger'd with you at your shop
To see the making of her carcanet,
And that to-morrow you will bring it home.
But here's a villain that would face me down
He met me on the mart, and that I beat him,
And charged him with a thousand marks in gold,
And that I did deny my wife and house.
Thou drunkard, thou, what didst thou mean by this?   10
DRO. E.   Say what you will, sir, but I know what I know;
That you beat me at the mart, I have your hand to show:
If the skin were parchment, and the blows you gave were
     ink,
Your own handwriting would tell you what I think.
ANT. E.   I think thou art an ass.
DRO. E.   Marry, so it doth appear
By the wrongs I suffer, and the blows I bear.
I should kick, being kick'd; and, being at that pass,
You would keep from my heels, and beware of an ass.
ANT. E.   You're sad, Signior Balthazar: pray God our cheer   20
May answer my good will and your good welcome here.
BAL.   I hold your dainties cheap, sir, and your welcome dear.
ANT. E.   O, Signior Balthazar, either at flesh or fish,
A table full of welcome makes scarce one dainty dish.
BAL.   Good meat, sir, is common: that every churl affords.
ANT. E.   And welcome more common; for that's nothing but
     words.

19

BAL.　Small cheer and great welcome makes a merry feast.

ANT. E.　Ay, to a niggardly host and more sparing guest:
But though my cates be mean, take them in good part;
Better cheer may you have, but not with better heart.　30
But, soft! my door is lock'd.—Go bid them let us in.

DRO. E.　Maud, Bridget, Marian, Cicely, Gillian, Ginn!

DRO. S. [*Within*]　Mome, malt-horse, capon, coxcomb, idiot, patch!
Either get thee from the door, or sit down at the hatch.
Dost thou conjure for wenches, that thou call'st for such store,
When one is one too many? Go get thee from the door.

DRO. E.　What patch is made our porter? My master stays in the street.

DRO. S. [*Within*]　Let him walk from whence he came, lest he catch cold on 's feet.

ANT. E.　Who talks within there? ho, open the door!

DRO. S. [*Within*]　Right, sir; I'll tell you when, an you'll tell me wherefore.　40

ANT. E.　Wherefore? for my dinner: I have not dined to-day.

DRO. S. [*Within*]　Nor to-day here you must not; come again when you may.

ANT. E.　What art thou that keepest me out from the house I owe?

DRO. S. [*Within*]　The porter for this time, sir, and my name is Dromio.

DRO. E.　O villain, thou hast stolen both mine office and my name!
The one ne'er got me credit, the other mickle blame.
If thou hadst been Dromio to-day in my place,
Thou wouldst have changed thy face for a name, or thy name for an ass.

LUCE. [*Within*]　What a coil is there, Dromio? who are those at the gate!

DRO. E.　Let my master in, Luce.　50

LUCE.　　　　　　　　　[*Within*]　'Faith, no; he comes too late;
And so tell your master.

DRO. E.　　　　　　　　　O Lord, I must laugh!
Have at you with a proverb;—Shall I set in my staff?

---

54 *Shall I set in my staff?*] "To set in one's staff" is a proverbial expression meaning "to make one's self at home."

LUCE. [*Within*]   Have at you with another; that's,—When? can
   you tell?
DRO. S. [*Within*]   If thy name be call'd Luce,—Luce, thou hast
   answer'd him well.
ANT. E.   Do you hear, you minion? you'll let us in, I hope?
LUCE. [*Within*]   I thought to have ask'd you.
DRO. S.   [*Within*]   And you said no.
DRO. E.   So, come, help: well struck! there was blow for blow.   60
ANT. E.   Thou baggage, let me in.
LUCE.   [*Within*]   Can you tell for whose sake?
DRO. E.   Master, knock the door hard.
LUCE.   [*Within*]   Let him knock till it ache.
ANT. E.   You'll cry for this, minion, if I beat the door down.
LUCE. [*Within*]   What needs all that, and a pair of stocks in the
   town?
ADR. [*Within*]   Who is that at the door that keeps all this noise?
DRO. S. [*Within*]   By my troth, your town is troubled with un-
   ruly boys.
ANT. E.   Are you there, wife? you might have come before.
ADR. [*Within*]   Your wife, sir knave! go get you from the door.   70
DRO. E.   If you went in pain, master, this "knave" would go sore.
ANG.   Here is neither cheer, sir, nor welcome: we would fain
   have either.
BAL.   In debating which was best, we shall part with neither.
DRO. E.   They stand at the door, master; bid them welcome
   hither.
ANT. E.   There is something in the wind, that we cannot get in.
DRO. E.   You would say so, master, if your garments were thin.
   Your cake here is warm within; you stand here in the cold:
   It would make a man mad as a buck, to be so bought and
     sold.
ANT. E.   Go fetch me something: I'll break ope the gate.
DRO. S. [*Within*]   Break any breaking here, and I'll break your
   knave's pate.   80
DRO. E.   A man may break a word with you, sir; and words are
   but wind;
   Ay, and break it in your face, so he break it not behind.

55 *When? can you tell?*] Another proverbial expression or catchword, used by way of par-
  rying an awkward question.
71 *If you went in pain, etc.*] A poor, quibbling echo of the application of the insulting
  word "knave" to the speaker's master: "You are a knave, so, if you felt pain, you would
  be a sore knave."
73 *part with*] From French "partir," "to go away;" "go away with," "obtain."
78 *bought and sold*] taken in, deceived.

DRO. S. [*Within*]   It seems thou want'st breaking: out upon thee, hind!

DRO. E.   Here's too much "out upon thee!" I pray thee, let me in.

DRO. S. [*Within*]   Ay, when fowls have no feathers, and fish have no fin.

ANT. E.   Well, I'll break in: go borrow me a crow.

DRO. E.   A crow without feather? Master, mean you so?
For a fish without a fin, there's a fowl without a feather:
If a crow help us in, sirrah, we'll pluck a crow together.

ANT. E.   Go get thee gone; fetch me an iron crow.   90

BAL.   Have patience, sir: O, let it not be so!
Herein you war against your reputation,
And draw within the compass of suspect
The unviolated honour of your wife.
Once this,—your long experience of her wisdom,
Her sober virtue, years, and modesty,
Plead on her part some cause to you unknown;
And doubt not, sir, but she will well excuse
Why at this time the doors are made against you.
Be ruled by me: depart in patience,   100
And let us to the Tiger all to dinner;
And about evening come yourself alone
To know the reason of this strange restraint.
If by strong hand you offer to break in
Now in the stirring passage of the day,
A vulgar comment will be made of it,
And that supposed by the common rout
Against your yet ungalled estimation,
That may with foul intrusion enter in,
And dwell upon your grave when you are dead;   110
For slander lives upon succession,
For ever housed where it gets possession.

ANT. E.   You have prevail'd: I will depart in quiet,
And, in despite of mirth, mean to be merry.

---

95 *Once this*] Once for all, in fine, to sum up. This usage is not uncommon, though rare. Malone proposed to read *Own this*.

99 *made against*] "barred against," a common provincial usage.

105–111 *Now . . . succession*] Now in the busy time of the day, when people are most about, adverse comments will be made by the crowd, and censure proceeding from the common people's suppositions, when it is aimed at your hitherto unblemished reputation, may get a firm footing, with all its foulness, and may adhere to your name when you are dead; for slander is never without heirs to keep up the estate.

114 *in despite of mirth*] in the absence of any just cause for mirth.

I know a wench of excellent discourse,
Pretty and witty; wild, and yet, too, gentle:
There will we dine. This woman that I mean,
My wife—but, I protest, without desert—
Hath oftentimes upbraided me withal:
To her will we to dinner. [*To* ANG.] Get you home,   120
And fetch the chain; by this I know 't is made:
Bring it, I pray you, to the Porpentine;
For there's the house: that chain will I bestow—
Be it for nothing but to spite my wife—
Upon mine hostess there: good sir, make haste.
Since mine own doors refuse to entertain me,
I'll knock elsewhere, to see if they'll disdain me.
ANG.   I'll meet you at that place some hour hence.
ANT. E.   Do so. This jest shall cost me some expense.

                                                     [*Exeunt.*

SCENE II. *The Same.*

Enter LUCIANA, *with* ANTIPHOLUS of Syracuse

LUC.   And may it be that you have quite forgot
    A husband's office? shall, Antipholus,
Even in the spring of love, thy love-springs rot?
    Shall love, in building, grow so ruinous?
If you did wed my sister for her wealth,
    Then for her wealth's sake use her with more kindness:
Or if you like elsewhere, do it by stealth,
    Muffle your false love with some show of blindness:
Let not my sister read it in your eye;
    Be not thy tongue thy own shame's orator;   10
Look sweet, speak fair, become disloyalty;
    Apparel vice like virtue's harbinger;
Bear a fair presence, though your heart be tainted;
    Teach sin the carriage of a holy saint;
Be secret-false: what need she be acquainted?
    What simple thief brags of his own attaint?
'T is double wrong, to truant with your bed,
    And let her read it in thy looks at board:
Shame hath a bastard fame, well managed;

---

3 *love-springs*] young shoots of love.
4 *Shall love, etc.*] Cf. *Sonnet* cxix, 11: "And *ruin'd love*, when it is *built* anew."
   Theobald substituted *ruinous* for *ruinate*, the obvious error of the Folio.

Ill deeds are doubled with an evil word. 20
Alas, poor women! make us but believe,
Being compact of credit, that you love us;
Though others have the arm, show us the sleeve;
We in your motion turn, and you may move us.
Then, gentle brother, get you in again;
Comfort my sister, cheer her, call her wife:
'T is holy sport, to be a little vain,
When the sweet breath of flattery conquers strife.
ANT. S.   Sweet mistress,—what your name is else, I know not,
Nor by what wonder you do hit of mine,— 30
Less in your knowledge and your grace you show not
Than our earth's wonder; more than earth divine
Teach me, dear creature, how to think and speak;
Lay open to my earthy-gross conceit,
Smother'd in errors, feeble, shallow, weak,
The folded meaning of your words' deceit.
Against my soul's pure truth why labour you
To make it wander in an unknown field?
Are you a god? would you create me new?
Transform me, then, and to your power I'll yield. 40
But if that I am I, then well I know
Your weeping sister is no wife of mine,
Nor to her bed no homage do I owe:
Far more, far more to you do I decline.
O, train me not, sweet mermaid, with thy note,
To drown me in thy sister's flood of tears:
Sing, siren, for thyself, and I will dote:
Spread o'er the silver waves thy golden hairs,
And as a bed I'll take them, and there lie;
And, in that glorious supposition, think 50
He gains by death that hath such means to die:
Let Love, being light, be drowned if she sink!
LUC.   What, are you mad, that you do reason so?
ANT. S.   Not mad, but mated; how, I do not know.
LUC.   It is a fault that springeth from your eye.
ANT. S.   For gazing on your beams, fair sun, being by.
LUC.   Gaze where you should, and that will clear your sight.
ANT. S.   As good to wink, sweet love, as look on night.

22 *compact of credit*] compounded, made up entirely, of credulity.
54 *Not mad, but mated*] The quibble on "mated" in the double sense of "bewildered" and "having a mate or partner," is common. Cf. V, i, 283, *infra*, and *T. of Shrew*, III, ii, 248, where "mated" and "mad" similarly figure together.

LUC. Why call you me love? call my sister so.
ANT. S. Thy sister's sister. 60
LUC. That's my sister.
ANT. S. No;
    It is thyself, mine own self's better part,
    Mine eye's clear eye, my dear heart's dearer heart,
    My food, my fortune, and my sweet hope's aim,
    My sole earth's heaven, and my heaven's claim.
LUC. All this my sister is, or else should be.
ANT. S. Call thyself sister, sweet, for I am thee.
    Thee will I love, and with thee lead my life:
    Thou hast no husband yet, nor I no wife. 70
    Give me thy hand.
LUC. O, soft, sir! hold you still:
    I'll fetch my sister, to get her good will.

                           [*Exit.*

Enter DROMIO of Syracuse

ANT. S. Why, how now, Dromio! where runn'st thou so fast?
DRO. S. Do you know me, sir? am I Dromio? am I your man? am I myself?
ANT. S. Thou art Dromio, thou art my man, thou art thyself.
DRO. S. I am an ass, I am a woman's man, and besides myself.
ANT. S. What woman's man? and how besides thyself?
DRO. S. Marry, sir, besides myself, I am due to a woman; one 80
    that claims me, one that haunts me, one that will have me.
ANT. S. What claim lays she to thee?
DRO. S. Marry, sir, such claim as you would lay to your horse;
    and she would have me as a beast: not that, I being a beast,
    she would have me; but that she, being a very beastly crea-
    ture, lays claim to me.
ANT. S. What is she?
DRO. S. A very reverent body; ay, such a one as a man may not
    speak of, without he say Sir-reverence. I have but lean luck
    in the match, and yet is she a wondrous fat marriage. 90
ANT. S. How dost thou mean a fat marriage?
DRO. S. Marry, sir, she's the kitchen-wench, and all grease; and
    I know not what use to put her to, but to make a lamp of her,
    and run from her by her own light. I warrant, her rags, and

66 *heaven's claim*] all that I claim of heaven.
68 *I am thee*] I identify myself with thee. Capell read, "I aim [*i.e.* mean] thee," dupli-
    cating "my sweet hope's aim" (l. 65); but the change does not seem necessary.
89 *Sir-reverence*] a vulgar corruption of "save" or "saving your reverence;" a derivative
    from the Latin, *salvâ reverentiâ, i.e.* "asking your pardon."

the tallow in them, will burn a Poland winter: if she lives till doomsday, she'll burn a week longer than the whole world.

ANT. S.　What complexion is she of?

DRO. S.　Swart, like my shoe, but her face nothing like so clean kept: for why she sweats; a man may go over shoes in the grime of it.　　　　　　　　　　　　　　　　　　　　　　　100

ANT. S.　That's a fault that water will mend.

DRO. S.　No, sir, 't is in grain; Noah's flood could not do it.

ANT. S.　What's her name?

DRO. S.　Nell, sir; but her name and three quarters, that's an ell and three quarters, will not measure her from hip to hip.

ANT. S.　Then she bears some breadth?

DRO. S.　No longer from head to foot than from hip to hip: she is spherical, like a globe; I could find out countries in her.

ANT. S.　In what part of her body stands Ireland?

DRO. S.　Marry, sir, in her buttocks: I found it out by the bogs.　110

ANT. S.　Where Scotland?

DRO. S.　I found it by the barrenness; hard in the palm of the hand.

ANT. S.　Where France?

DRO. S.　In her forehead; armed and reverted, making war against her heir.

ANT. S.　Where England?

DRO. S.　I looked for the chalky cliffs, but I could find no whiteness in them; but I guess it stood in her chin, by the salt rheum that ran between France and it.　　　　　　　　　　　120

ANT. S.　Where Spain?

DRO. S.　'Faith, I saw it not; but I felt it hot in her breath.

ANT. S.　Where America, the Indies?

DRO. S.　Oh, sir, upon her nose, all o'er embellished with rubies, carbuncles, sapphires, declining their rich aspect to the hot breath of Spain; who sent whole armadoes of caracks to be ballast at her nose.

ANT. S.　Where stood Belgia, the Netherlands?

DRO. S.　Oh, sir, I did not look so low. To conclude, this drudge, or diviner, laid claim to me; called me Dromio; swore I was　130 assured to her; told me what privy marks I had about me, as,

---

116 *heir*] The Second Folio reads *haire*. The quibble refers to the civil war progressing in France at the date of the production of the play, when Henry of Navarre, whom Englishmen regarded as the rightful heir to the French throne, was fighting for the succession.

127 *ballast*] ballasted, loaded.

the mark of my shoulder, the mole in my neck, the great
wart on my left arm, that I, amazed, ran from her as a witch:
And, I think, if my breast had not been made of faith, and
    my heart of steel,
She had transform'd me to a curtal dog, and made me turn
    i' the wheel.

ANT. S.   Go hie thee presently, post to the road:
An if the wind blow any way from shore,
I will not harbour in this town to-night:
If any bark put forth, come to the mart,
Where I will walk till thou return to me.   140
If every one knows us, and we know none,
'T is time, I think, to trudge, pack, and be gone.

DRO. S.   As from a bear a man would run for life,
So fly I from her that would be my wife.

                                              [*Exit.*

ANT. S.   There's none but witches do inhabit here;
And therefore 't is high time that I were hence.
She that doth call me husband, even my soul
Doth for a wife abhor. But her fair sister,
Possess'd with such a gentle sovereign grace,
Of such enchanting presence and discourse,   150
Hath almost made me traitor to myself:
But, lest myself be guilty to self-wrong,
I'll stop mine ears against the mermaid's song.

Enter ANGELO *with the chain*

ANG.   Master Antipholus, —
ANT. S.   Ay, that's my name.
ANG.   I know it well, sir: lo, here is the chain.
I thought to have ta'en you at the Porpentine:
The chain unfinish'd made me stay thus long.
ANT. S.   What is your will that I shall do with this?
ANG.   What please yourself, sir: I have made it for you.   160
ANT. S.   Made it for me, sir! I bespoke it not.
ANG.   Not once, nor twice, but twenty times you have.
Go home with it, and please your wife withal;
And soon at supper-time I'll visit you,
And then receive my money for the chain.
ANT. S.   I pray you, sir, receive the money now,
For fear you ne'er see chain nor money more.

---

135 *curtal . . . wheel*] dog with a docked tail that worked the turnspit in the kitchen.

ANG.   You are a merry man, sir: fare you well.

[*Exit.*

ANT. S.   What I should think of this, I cannot tell:
But this I think, there's no man is so vain   170
That would refuse so fair an offer'd chain.
I see a man here needs not live by shifts,
When in the streets he meets such golden gifts.
I'll to the mart, and there for Dromio stay:
If any ship put out, then straight away.

[*Exit.*

ACT IV.

SCENE I. *A Public Place.*

Enter Second Merchant, ANGELO, *and an* Officer

SECOND MERCHANT.   You know since Pentecost the sum is due,
    And since I have not much importuned you;
    Nor now I had not, but that I am bound
    To Persia, and want guilders for my voyage:
    Therefore make present satisfaction,
    Or I'll attach you by this officer.
ANG.   Even just the sum that I do owe to you
    Is growing to me by Antipholus;
    And in the instant that I met with you
    He had of me a chain: at five o'clock   10
    I shall receive the money for the same.
    Pleaseth you walk with me down to his house,
    I will discharge my bond, and thank you too.

Enter ANTIPHOLUS of Ephesus *and* DROMIO of Ephesus *from the
    courtezan's*

OFF.   That labour may you save: see where he comes.
ANT. E.   While I go to the goldsmith's house, go thou
    And buy a rope's end: that will I bestow
    Among my wife and her confederates,
    For locking me out of my doors by day.
    But, soft! I see the goldsmith. Get thee gone;
    Buy thou a rope, and bring it home to me.   20
DRO. E.   I buy a thousand pound a year: I buy a rope.

                                  [*Exit.*

  4 *guilders*] See note on I, i, 8, *supra.*
  8 *growing*] accruing. Cf. IV, iv, 128 *et seq., infra.*
21 *I buy . . . rope*] Dromio means that the purchase of a rope, wherewith to execute his mas-
    ter's scheme of vengeance, is as grateful to him as the requisition of a large annuity.

ANT. E.　A man is well holp up that trusts to you:
　　　　I promised your presence and the chain;
　　　　But neither chain nor goldsmith came to me.
　　　　Belike you thought our love would last too long,
　　　　If it were chain'd together, and therefore came not.
ANG.　Saving your merry humour, here's the note
　　　　How much your chain weighs to the utmost carat,
　　　　The fineness of the gold, and chargeful fashion,
　　　　Which doth amount to three odd ducats more　　　　　　30
　　　　Than I stand debted to this gentleman:
　　　　I pray you, see him presently discharged,
　　　　For he is bound to sea, and stays but for it.
ANT. E.　I am not furnish'd with the present money;
　　　　Besides, I have some business in the town.
　　　　Good signior, take the stranger to my house,
　　　　And with you take the chain, and bid my wife
　　　　Disburse the sum on the receipt thereof:
　　　　Perchance I will be there as soon as you.
ANG.　Then you will bring the chain to her yourself?　　　40
ANT. E.　No; bear it with you, lest I come not time enough.
ANG.　Well, sir, I will. Have you the chain about you?
ANT. E.　And if I have not, sir, I hope you have;
　　　　Or else you may return without your money.
ANG.　Nay, come, I pray you, sir, give me the chain:
　　　　Both wind and tide stays for this gentleman,
　　　　And I, to blame, have held him here too long.
ANT. E.　Good Lord! you use this dalliance to excuse
　　　　Your breach of promise to the Porpentine.
　　　　I should have chid you for not bringing it,　　　　　50
　　　　But, like a shrew, you first begin to brawl.
SEC. MER.　The hour steals on; I pray you, sir, dispatch.
ANG.　You hear how he importunes me;—the chain!
ANT. E.　Why, give it to my wife, and fetch your money.
ANG.　Come, come, you know I gave it you even now.
　　　　Either send the chain, or send me by some token.
ANT. E.　Fie, now you run this humour out of breath.
　　　　Come, where's the chain? I pray you, let me see it.
SEC. MER.　My business cannot brook this dalliance.
　　　　Good sir, say whether you'll answer me or no:　　　60
　　　　If not, I'll leave him to the officer.
ANT. E.　I answer you! what should I answer you?
ANG.　The money that you owe me for the chain.

56 *send me by some token*] send me furnished with some token by way of warrant.

ANT. E.   I owe you none till I receive the chain.

ANG.   You know I gave it you half an hour since.

ANT. E.   You gave me none: you wrong me much to say so.

ANG.   You wrong me more, sir, in denying it:
     Consider how it stands upon my credit.

SEC. MER.   Well, officer, arrest him at my suit.

OFF.   I do; and charge you in the duke's name to obey me.   70

ANG.   This touches me in reputation.
     Either consent to pay this sum for me,
     Or I attach you by this officer.

ANT. E.   Consent to pay thee that I never had!
     Arrest me, foolish fellow, if thou darest.

ANG.   Here is thy fee; arrest him, officer.
     I would not spare my brother in this case,
     If he should scorn me so apparently.

OFF.   I do arrest you, sir: you hear the suit.

ANT. E.   I do obey thee till I give thee bail.   80
     But, sirrah, you shall buy this sport as dear
     As all the metal in your shop will answer.

ANG.   Sir, sir, I shall have law in Ephesus,
     To your notorious shame; I doubt it not.

Enter DROMIO *of Syracuse, from the bay*

DRO. S.   Master, there is a bark of Epidamnum
     That stays but till her owner comes aboard,
     And then, sir, she bears away. Our fraughtage, sir,
     I have convey'd aboard; and I have bought
     The oil, the balsamum, and aqua-vitæ.
     The ship is in her trim; the merry wind   90
     Blows fair from land: they stay for nought at all
     But for their owner, master, and yourself.

ANT. E.   How now! a madman! Why, thou peevish sheep,
     What ship of Epidamnum stays for me?

DRO. S.   A ship you sent me to, to hire waftage.

ANT. E.   Thou drunken slave, I sent thee for a rope,
     And told thee to what purpose and what end.

DRO. S.   You sent me for a rope's end as soon:
     You sent me to the bay, sir, for a bark.

ANT. E.   I will debate this matter at more leisure,   100
     And teach your ears to list me with more heed.
     To Adriana, villain, hie thee straight:

98 *a rope's end*] Steevens completed the metre by inserting *sir* after *end*, but Malone
   deemed *rope's* a dissyllable.

Give her this key, and tell her, in the desk
That's cover'd o'er with Turkish tapestry
There is a purse of ducats; let her send it:
Tell her I am arrested in the street,
And that shall bail me: hie thee, slave, be gone!
On, officer, to prison till it come.

        [*Exeunt* Sec. Merchant, ANGELO, Officer, *and* ANT. E.

DRO. S.   To Adriana! that is where we dined,
Where Dowsabel did claim me for her husband: 110
She is too big, I hope, for me to compass.
Thither I must, although against my will,
For servants must their masters' minds fulfil.

                          [*Exit.*

SCENE II. *The House of Antipholus of Ephesus.*

Enter ADRIANA *and* LUCIANA

ADR.   Ah, Luciana, did he tempt thee so?
       Mightst thou perceive austerely in his eye
   That he did plead in earnest? yea or no?
       Look'd he or red or pale, or sad or merrily?
   What observation madest thou, in this case,
     Of his heart's meteors tilting in his face?
LUC.   First he denied you had in him no right.
ADR.   He meant he did me none; the more my spite.
LUC.   Then swore he that he was a stranger here.
ADR.   And true he swore, though yet forsworn he were.   10
LUC.   Then pleaded I for you.
ADR.   And what said he?
LUC.   That love I begg'd for you he begg'd of me.
ADR.   With what persuasion did he tempt thy love?
LUC.   With words that in an honest suit might move,
   First he did praise my beauty, then my speech.
ADR.   Didst speak him fair?
LUC.   Have patience, I beseech.
ADR.   I cannot, nor I will not, hold me still;
   My tongue, though not my heart, shall have his will.   20
   He is deformed, crooked, old, and sere,
   Ill-faced, worse bodied, shapeless everywhere;
   Vicious, ungentle, foolish, blunt, unkind;

110 *Dowsabel*] A common name for a country wench.

Stigmatical in making, worse in mind.
LUC.   Who would be jealous, then, of such a one?
No evil lost is wail'd when it is gone.
ADR.   Ah, but I think him better than I say,
And yet would herein others' eyes were worse.
Far from her nest the lapwing cries away:
My heart prays for him, though my tongue do curse.   30

Enter DROMIO of Syracuse

DRO. S.   Here! go; the desk, the purse! sweet, now, make haste.
LUC.   How hast thou lost thy breath?
DRO. S.   By running fast.
ADR.   Where is thy master, Dromio? is he well?
DRO. S.   No, he's in Tartar limbo, worse than hell.
A devil in an everlasting garment hath him;
One whose hard heart is button'd up with steel;
A fiend, a fury, pitiless and rough,
A wolf, nay, worse; a fellow all in buff;
A back-friend, a shoulder-clapper, one that countermands   40
The passages of alleys, creeks, and narrow lands;
A hound that runs counter, and yet draws dry-foot well;
One that, before the Judgment, carries poor souls to hell.
ADR.   Why, man, what is the matter?
DRO. S.   I do not know the matter: he is 'rested on the case.
ADR.   What, is he arrested? Tell me at whose suit.
DRO. S.   I know not at whose suit he is arrested well;
But he's in a suit of buff which 'rested him, that can I tell.
Will you send him, mistress, redemption, the money in his
desk?
ADR.   Go fetch it, sister. [*Exit* LUCIANA.] This I wonder at,   50
That he, unknown to me, should be in debt.

---

29 *Far from her nest, etc.*] A very common proverbial expression.
35 *in Tartar limbo*] in gaol.
36 A *devil, etc.*] a bailiff or sergeant, whose buff jerkin was usually made of stuff called
"durance," which was reputed never to wear out.
38 *fury*] Theobald's alteration of the old reading *fairy*, which is so often found in the
sense of elf or hobgoblin that it might well be retained.
41 *lands*] Possibly *lands* is here identical with "launds," *i.e.* "glades." The rhyme forbids
the acceptance of the alternative reading *lanes*.
42 A *hound that runs counter*] To "run counter" is to run backwards or on a false scent.
Here there is a punning reference to the *counter, i.e.* prison whither the sergeant carried his victims. To "draw dry-foot" is to follow the scent on dry ground.
43 *hell*] a cant term for "prison."

Tell me, was he arrested on a band?

DRO. S.   Not on a band, but on a stronger thing;
 A chain, a chain! Do you not hear it ring?

ADR.   What, the chain?

DRO. S.   No, no, the bell: 't is time that I were gone:
 It was two ere I left him, and now the clock strikes one.

ADR.   The hours come back! that did I never hear.

DRO. S.   O, yes; if any hour meet a sergeant, 'a turns back for
 very fear.

ADR.   As if Time were in debt! how fondly dost thou reason! 60

DRO. S.   Time is a very bankrupt, and owes more than he's worth
 to season.
 Nay, he's a thief too: have you not heard men say,
 That Time comes stealing on by night and day?
 If Time be in debt and theft, and sergeant in the way,
 Hath he not reason to turn back an hour in a day?

Re-enter LUCIANA *with a purse*

ADR.   Go, Dromio; there's the money, bear it straight;
 And bring thy master home immediately.
 Come, sister: I am press'd down with conceit,—
 Conceit, my comfort and my injury.

           [*Exeunt.*

SCENE III. A *Public Place.*

Enter ANTIPHOLUS of Syracuse

ANT. S.   There's not a man I meet but doth salute me
 As if I were their well-acquainted friend;
 And every one doth call me by my name.
 Some tender money to me; some invite me;
 Some other give me thanks for kindnesses;
 Some offer me commodities to buy:
 Even now a tailor call'd me in his shop,
 And show'd me silks that he had bought for me,
 And therewithal took measure of my body.
 Sure, these are but imaginary wiles, 10

---

52 *band*] bond. This form of the word is common, and the quibbling use of it, though
 feeble, is intelligible.
61 *season*] opportunity.
68 *conceit*] anxious thought.

And Lapland sorcerers inhabit here.

Enter DROMIO of Syracuse

DRO. S.   Master, here's the gold you sent me for. What, have
   you got the picture of old Adam new-apparelled?
ANT. S.   What gold is this? what Adam dost thou mean?
DRO. S.   Not that Adam that kept the Paradise, but that Adam
   that keeps the prison: he that goes in the calf's skin that was
   killed for the Prodigal; he that came behind you, sir, like an
   evil angel, and bid you forsake your liberty.
ANT. S.   I understand thee not.
DRO. S.   No? why, 't is a plain case: he that went, like a base-viol,   20
   in a case of leather; the man, sir, that, when gentlemen are
   tired, gives them a sob, and 'rests them; he, sir, that takes pity
   on decayed men, and gives them suits of durance; he that
   sets up his rest to do more exploits with his mace than a
   morris-pike.
ANT. S.   What, thou meanest an officer?
DRO. S.   Ay, sir, the sergeant of the band; he that brings any man
   to answer it that breaks his band; one that thinks a man al-
   ways going to bed, and says, "God give you good rest!"
ANT. S.   Well, sir, there rest in your foolery. Is there any ship   30
   puts forth to-night? may we be gone?
DRO. S.   Why, sir, I brought you word an hour since, that the
   bark Expedition put forth to-night; and then were you hin-
   dered by the sergeant, to tarry for the hoy Delay. Here are
   the angels that you sent for to deliver you.
ANT. S.   The fellow is distract, and so am I;
   And here we wander in illusions:
   Some blessed power deliver us from hence!

Enter a Courtezan

COUR.   Well met, well met, Master Antipholus,

11 *Lapland sorcerers*] The inhabitants of Lapland were commonly reputed to be sorcerers and witches. "Lapland witches," a common expression in Elizabethan writers,
   figures in Milton's *Paradise Lost*, II, 665.
12–13 *have you . . . old Adam*] Theobald reads, *have you got rid of*, etc. Dromio's inquiry
   is clearly equivalent to "What has become of the sergeant?" Dromio is asking in
   quibbling fashion where the stout corporeal presence of old leather-clad Adam, as he
   playfully calls the sergeant, has got to.
22 *gives . . . sob*] causes them a convulsive sigh. This is the reading of the Folios, which
   Rowe changed to *fob*, assigning to that word the unsupported meaning of "tap," or
   "light blow."
23 *durance*] See note on IV, ii, 36. There is a quibble on the sense of *durance*, *i.e.*
   prison. The word also means cloth that does not wear out.

I see, sir, you have found the goldsmith now: 40
Is that the chain you promised me to-day?

ANT. S.   Satan, avoid! I charge thee, tempt me not.

DRO. S.   Master, is this Mistress Satan?

ANT. S.   It is the devil.

DRO. S.   Nay, she is worse, she is the devil's dam; and here she
comes in the habit of a light wench: and thereof comes that
the wenches say, "God damn me;" that's as much to say,
"God make me a light wench." It is written, they appear to
men like angels of light: light is an effect of fire, and fire will
burn; ergo, light wenches will burn. Come not near her.   50

COUR.   Your man and you are marvellous merry, sir. Will you go
with me? We'll mend our dinner here?

DRO. S.   Master, if you do, expect spoon-meat; or bespeak a long
spoon.

ANT. S.   Why, Dromio?

DRO. S.   Marry, he must have a long spoon that must eat with
the devil.

ANT. S.   Avoid then, fiend! what tell'st thou me of supping?
Thou art, as you are all, a sorceress:
I conjure thee to leave me and be gone.   60

COUR.   Give me the ring of mine you had at dinner,
Or, for my diamond, the chain you promised,
And I'll be gone, sir, and not trouble you.

DRO. S.   Some devils ask but the parings of one's nail,
A rush, a hair, a drop of blood, a pin,
A nut, a cherry-stone;
But she, more covetous, would have a chain.
Master, be wise: an if you give it her,
The devil will shake her chain, and fright us with it.

COUR.   I pray you, sir, my ring, or else the chain: 70
I hope you do not mean to cheat me so.

ANT. S.   Avaunt, thou witch! Come, Dromio, let us go.

DRO. S.   "Fly pride," says the peacock: mistress, that you know.
                    [*Exeunt* ANT. S. *and* DRO. S.

COUR.   Now, out of doubt Antipholus is mad,
Else would he never so demean himself.
A ring he hath of mine worth forty ducats,
And for the same he promised me a chain:
Both one and other he denies me now.
The reason that I gather he is mad,

---

52 *We'll mend, etc.*] We'll improve, make some addition to.
53–54 *a long spoon*] This proverb is alluded to again in the *Tempest*, II, ii, 103.

Besides this present instance of his rage,   80
Is a mad tale he told to-day at dinner,
Of his own doors being shut against his entrance.
Belike his wife, acquainted with his fits,
On purpose shut the doors against his way.
My way is now to hie home to his house,
And tell his wife that, being lunatic,
He rush'd into my house, and took perforce
My ring away. This course I fittest choose;
For forty ducats is too much to lose.

> [*Exit.*

SCENE IV. *A Street.*

Enter ANTIPHOLUS *of Ephesus and the* Officer

ANT. E.   Fear me not, man; I will not break away:
I'll give thee, ere I leave thee, so much money,
To warrant thee, as I am 'rested for.
My wife is in a wayward mood to-day,
And will not lightly trust the messenger.
That I should be attach'd in Ephesus,
I tell you, 't will sound harshly in her ears.

Enter DROMIO *of Ephesus with a rope's-end*

Here comes my man; I think he brings the money.
How now, sir! have you that I sent you for?
DRO. E.   Here's that, I warrant you, will pay them all.   10
ANT. E.   But where's the money?
DRO. E.   Why, sir, I gave the money for the rope.
ANT. E.   Five hundred ducats, villain, for a rope?
DRO. E.   I'll serve you, sir, five hundred at the rate.
ANT. E.   To what end did I bid thee hie thee home?
DRO. E.   To a rope's-end, sir; and to that end am I returned.
ANT. E.   And to that end, sir, I will welcome you.

> [*Beating him.*

OFF.   Good sir, be patient.
DRO. E.   Nay, 't is for me to be patient; I am in adversity.
OFF.   Good now, hold thy tongue.   20
DRO. E.   Nay, rather persuade him to hold his hands.
ANT. E.   Thou whoreson, senseless villain!
DRO. E.   I would I were senseless, sir, that I might not feel your
blows.

ANT. E.   Thou art sensible in nothing but blows, and so is an ass.
DRO. E.   I am an ass, indeed; you may prove it by my long ears.
I have served him from the hour of my nativity to this in-
stant, and have nothing at his hands for my service but
blows. When I am cold, he heats me with beating; when I
am warm, he cools me with beating: I am waked with it   30
when I sleep; raised with it when I sit; driven out of doors
with it when I go from home; welcomed home with it when
I return: nay, I bear it on my shoulders, as a beggar wont her
brat; and, I think, when he hath lamed me, I shall beg with
it from door to door.
ANT. E.   Come, go along; my wife is coming yonder.

Enter ADRIANA, LUCIANA, *the* Courtezan, *and* PINCH

DRO. E.   Mistress, "respice finem," respect your end; or rather,
the prophecy like the parrot, "beware the rope's-end."
ANT. E.   Wilt thou still talk?
                                                    [*Beating him.*
COUR.   How say you now? is not your husband mad?   40
ADR.   His incivility confirms no less.
Good Doctor Pinch, you are a conjurer;
Establish him in his true sense again,
And I will please you what you will demand.
LUC.   Alas, how fiery and how sharp he looks!
COUR.   Mark how he trembles in his ecstasy!
PINCH.   Give me your hand, and let me feel your pulse.
ANT. E.   There is my hand, and let it feel your ear.
                                                    [*Striking him.*
PINCH.   I charge thee, Satan, housed within this man,
To yield possession to my holy prayers,   50
And to thy state of darkness hie thee straight:
I conjure thee by all the saints in heaven!
ANT. E.   Peace, doting wizard, peace! I am not mad.
ADR.   O, that thou wert not, poor distressed soul!
ANT. E.   You minion, you, are these your customers?
Did this companion with the saffron face
Revel and feast it at my house to-day,
Whilst upon me the guilty doors were shut,
And I denied to enter in my house?
ADR.   O husband, God doth know you dined at home;   60

       Where would you had remain'd until this time,
       Free from these slanders and this open shame!

ANT. E.   Dined at home! Thou villain, what sayest thou?

DRO. E.   Sir, sooth to say, you did not dine at home.

ANT. E.   Were not my doors lock'd up, and I shut out?

DRO. E.   Perdie, your doors were lock'd, and you shut out.

ANT. E.   And did not she herself revile me there?

DRO. E.   Sans fable, she herself reviled you there.

ANT. E.   Did not her kitchen-maid rail, taunt, and scorn me?

DRO. E.   Certes, she did; the kitchen-vestal scorn'd you.   70

ANT. E.   And did not I in rage depart from thence?

DRO. E.   In verity you did; my bones bear witness,
       That since have felt the vigour of his rage.

ADR.   Is 't good to soothe him in these contraries?

PINCH.   It is no shame: the fellow finds his vein,
       And, yielding to him, humours well his frenzy.

ANT. E.   Thou hast suborn'd the goldsmith to arrest me

ADR.   Alas, I sent you money to redeem you,
       By Dromio here, who came in haste for it.

DRO. E.   Money by me! heart and good-will you might;   80
       But surely, master, not a rag of money.

ANT. E.   Went'st not thou to her for a purse of ducats?

ADR.   He came to me, and I deliver'd it.

LUC.   And I am witness with her that she did.

DRO. E.   God and the rope-maker bear me witness
       That I was sent for nothing but a rope!

PINCH.   Mistress, both man and master is possess'd;
       I know it by their pale and deadly looks:
       They must be bound, and laid in some dark room.

ANT. E.   Say, wherefore didst thou lock me forth to-day?   90
       And why dost thou deny the bag of gold?

ADR.   I did not, gentle husband, lock thee forth.

DRO. E.   And, gentle master, I received no gold;
       But I confess, sir, that we were lock'd out.

ADR.   Dissembling villain, thou speak'st false in both.

ANT. E.   Dissembling harlot, thou art false in all,
       And art confederate with a damned pack
       To make a loathsome abject scorn of me:
       But with these nails I'll pluck out these false eyes,
       That would behold in me this shameful sport.   100

Enter three or four, and offer to bind him. He strives

ADR.   O, bind him, bind him! let him not come near me.

PINCH. More company! The fiend is strong within him.

LUC. Ay me, poor man, how pale and wan he looks!

ANT. E. What, will you murder me? Thou gaoler, thou,
I am thy prisoner: wilt thou suffer them
To make a rescue?

OFF. Masters, let him go:
He is my prisoner, and you shall not have him.

PINCH. Go bind this man, for he is frantic too.
[*They offer to bind* DRO. E.

ADR. What wilt thou do, thou peevish officer? 110
Hast thou delight to see a wretched man
Do outrage and displeasure to himself?

OFF. He is my prisoner: if I let him go,
The debt he owes will be required of me.

ADR. I will discharge thee ere I go from thee:
Bear me forthwith unto his creditor,
And, knowing how the debt grows, I will pay it.
Good master doctor, see him safe convey'd
Home to my house. O most unhappy day!

ANT. E. O most unhappy strumpet! 120

DRO. E. Master, I am here enter'd in bond for you.

ANT. E. Out on thee, villain! wherefore dost thou mad me?

DRO. E. Will you be bound for nothing? be mad, good master:
cry, The devil!

LUC. God help, poor souls, how idly do they talk!

ADR. Go bear him hence. Sister, go you with me.
[*Exeunt all but* ADRIANA, LUCIANA, Officer *and* Courtezan.
Say now; whose suit is he arrested at?

OFF. One Angelo, a goldsmith: do you know him?

ADR. I know the man. What is the sum he owes?

OFF. Two hundred ducats. 130

ADR. Say, how grows it due?

OFF. Due for a chain your husband had of him.

ADR. He did bespeak a chain for me, but had it not.

COUR. When as your husband, all in rage, to-day
Came to my house, and took away my ring,—
The ring I saw upon his finger now,—
Straight after did I meet him with a chain.

ADR. It may be so, but I did never see it.
Come, gaoler, bring me where the goldsmith is:
I long to know the truth hereof at large. 140

Enter ANTIPHOLUS *of Syracuse with his rapier drawn, and*
        DROMIO *of Syracuse*

LUC.   God, for thy mercy! they are loose again.
ADR.   And come with naked swords.
        Let's call more help to have them bound again.
OFF.   Away! they'll kill us.
                    [*Exeunt all but* ANT. S. *and* DRO. S.
ANT. S.   I see these witches are afraid of swords.
DRO. S.   She that would be your wife now ran from you.
ANT. S.   Come to the Centaur; fetch our stuff from thence:
        I long that we were safe and sound aboard.
DRO. S.   Faith, stay here this night; they will surely do us no
        harm: you saw they speak us fair, give us gold: methinks they   150
        are such a gentle nation, that, but for the mountain of mad
        flesh that claims marriage of me, I could find in my heart to
        stay here still, and turn witch.
ANT. S.   I will not stay to-night for all the town;
        Therefore away, to get our stuff aboard.
                                        [*Exeunt.*

---

155 *stuff*] baggage. Shakespeare uses the word in this sense only here, in V, i, 412, *infra*,
    and in *Pericles*, IV, ii, 19. It appears in W. W.'s translation of Plautus' *Menæchmi:*
    "Ile go strait to the inne, and deliver up my accounts, and all your *stuffe*."

ACT V.

SCENE I. *A Street Before a Priory.*

Enter Second Merchant *and* ANGELO

ANGELO.   I am sorry, sir, that I have hinder'd you;
    But, I protest, he had the chain of me,
    Though most dishonestly he doth deny it.
SEC. MER.   How is the man esteem'd here in the city?
ANG.   Of very reverent reputation, sir,
    Of credit infinite, highly beloved,
    Second to none that lives here in the city:
    His word might bear my wealth at any time.
SEC. MER.   Speak softly: yonder, as I think, he walks.

Enter ANTIPHOLUS *of Syracuse and* DROMIO *of Syracuse*

ANG.   'T is so; and that self chain about his neck,   10
    Which he forswore most monstrously to have.
    Good sir, draw near to me, I'll speak to him;
    Signior Antipholus, I wonder much
    That you would put me to this shame and trouble;
    And, not without some scandal to yourself,
    With circumstance and oaths so to deny
    This chain which now you wear so openly:
    Beside the charge, the shame, imprisonment,
    You have done wrong to this my honest friend;
    Who, but for staying on our controversy,   20
    Had hoisted sail and put to sea to-day:
    This chain you had of me; can you deny it?
ANT. S.   I think I had; I never did deny it.
SEC. MER.   Yes, that you did, sir, and forswore it too.
ANT. S.   Who heard me to deny it or forswear it?
SEC. MER.   These ears of mine, thou know'st, did hear thee.
    Fie on thee, wretch! 't is pity that thou livest

To walk where any honest men resort.
ANT. S.   Thou art a villain to impeach me thus:
    I'll prove mine honour and mine honesty   30
    Against thee presently, if thou darest stand.
SEC. MER.   I dare, and do defy thee for a villain.

                                    [They draw.

Enter ADRIANA, LUCIANA, *the* Courtezan, *and others*

ADR.   Hold, hurt him not, for God's sake! he is mad.
    Some get within him, take his sword away:
    Bind Dromio too, and bear them to my house.
DRO. S.   Run, master, run; for God's sake, take a house!
    This is some priory. In, or we are spoiled!
                [Exeunt ANT. S. *and* DRO. S. *to the Priory.*

Enter the Lady Abbess

ABB.   Be quiet, people. Wherefore throng you hither?
ADR.   To fetch my poor distracted husband hence.
    Let us come in, that we may bind him fast,   40
    And bear him home for his recovery.
ANG.   I knew he was not in his perfect wits.
SEC. MER.   I am sorry now that I did draw on him.
ABB.   How long hath this possession held the man?
ADR.   This week he hath been heavy, sour, sad,
    And much different from the man he was;
    But till this afternoon his passion
    Ne'er break into extremity of rage.
ABB.   Hath he not lost much wealth by wreck of sea?
    Buried some dear friend? Hath not else his eye   50
    Stray'd his affection in unlawful love?
    A sin prevailing much in youthful men,
    Who give their eyes the liberty of gazing.
    Which of these sorrows is he subject to?
ADR.   To none of these, except it be the last;
    Namely, some love that drew him oft from home.
ABB.   You should for that have reprehended him.
ADR.   Why, so I did.
ABB.   Ay, but not rough enough.

34 *within him*] at close quarters with him.
36 *take a house*] enter, as in the phrase "a dog takes the water."
46 *much*] The Second Folio improves the metre by reading *much much*. The reading is
    worth adoption.
51 *Stray'd his affection*] Caused to stray, led astray; the transitive use of the word is ex-
    tremely rare, if not unique.

ADR. As roughly as my modesty would let me.   60
ABB. Haply, in private.
ADR.   And in assemblies too.
ABB. Ay, but not enough.
ADR. It was the copy of our conference:
    In bed, he slept not for my urging it;
    At board, he fed not for my urging it;
    Alone, it was the subject of my theme;
    In company I often glanced it;
    Still did I tell him it was vile and bad.
ABB. And thereof came it that the man was mad.   70
    The venom clamours of a jealous woman
    Poisons more deadly than a mad dog's tooth.
    It seems his sleeps were hinder'd by thy railing:
    And thereof comes it that his head is light.
    Thou say'st his meat was sauced with thy upbraidings:
    Unquiet meals make ill digestions;
    Thereof the raging fire of fever bred;
    And what's a fever but a fit of madness?
    Thou say'st his sports were hinder'd by thy brawls:
    Sweet recreation barr'd, what doth ensue   80
    But moody and dull melancholy,
    Kinsman to grim and comfortless despair;
    And at her heels a huge infectious troop
    Of pale distemperatures and foes to life?
    In food, in sport, and life-preserving rest
    To be disturb'd, would mad or man or beast:
    The consequence is, then, thy jealous fits
    Have scared thy husband from the use of wits.
LUC. She never reprehended him but mildly,
    When he demean'd himself rough, rude, and wildly.   90
    Why bear you these rebukes, and answer not?
ADR. She did betray me to my own reproof.
    Good people, enter, and lay hold on him.
ABB. No, not a creature enters in my house.
ADR. Then let your servants bring my husband forth.
ABB. Neither: he took this place for sanctuary,
    And it shall privilege him from your hands

64 *copy*] repeated theme.
71 *venom*] The noun is constantly used adjectivally for "venomous."
81 *moody, etc.*] The line is defective. Suggested interpolations are "sadness" or "mad-
  ness" after "moody," of which the latter is the more reasonable. Others insert "mop-
  ing" after "moody," or substitute "dull-visaged" for "dull."

Till I have brought him to his wits again,
Or lose my labour in assaying it.

ADR.   I will attend my husband, be his nurse,   100
Diet his sickness, for it is my office,
And will have no attorney but myself;
And therefore let me have him home with me.

ABB.   Be patient; for I will not let him stir
Till I have used the approved means I have,
With wholesome syrups, drugs and holy prayers,
To make of him a formal man again:
It is a branch and parcel of mine oath,
A charitable duty of my order.
Therefore depart, and leave him here with me.   110

ADR.   I will not hence, and leave my husband here:
And ill it doth beseem your holiness
To separate the husband and the wife.

ABB.   Be quiet, and depart: thou shalt not have him.

                                           [Exit.

LUC.   Complain unto the Duke of this indignity.

ADR.   Come, go: I will fall prostrate at his feet,
And never rise until my tears and prayers
Have won his Grace to come in person hither,
And take perforce my husband from the abbess.

SEC. MER.   By this, I think, the dial points at five: 120
Anon, I'm sure, the Duke himself in person
Comes this way to the melancholy vale,
The place of death and sorry execution,
Behind the ditches of the abbey here.

ANG.   Upon what cause?

SEC. MER.   To see a reverend Syracusian merchant,
Who put unluckily into this bay
Against the laws and statutes of this town,
Beheaded publicly for his offence.

ANG.   See where they come: we will behold his death.   130

LUC.   Kneel to the Duke before he pass the abbey.

Enter DUKE, *attended;* ÆGEON *bareheaded; with the* Headsman
    and other Officers

DUKE.   Yet once again proclaim it publicly,
If any friend will pay the sum for him,

---

107 *formal*] in a normal state of mind, sane. Cf. *Meas. for Meas.*, V, i, 236: "Poor *infor-*
    mal women," *i.e.* women out of their senses.
123 *death*] The Third Folio's correction of the First and Second Folios' reading *depth.*

He shall not die; so much we tender him.
ADR.   Justice, most sacred Duke, against the abbess!
DUKE.   She is a virtuous and a reverend lady:
    It cannot be that she hath done thee wrong.
ADR.   May it please your Grace, Antipholus my husband,—
    Whom I made lord of me and all I had,
    At your important letters,—this ill day   140
    A most outrageous fit of madness took him;
    That desperately he hurried through the street,—
    With him his bondman, all as mad as he,—
    Doing displeasure to the citizens
    By rushing in their houses, bearing thence
    Rings, jewels, any thing his rage did like.
    Once did I get him bound, and sent him home,
    Whilst to take order for the wrongs I went,
    That here and there his fury had committed.
    Anon, I wot not by what strong escape,   150
    He broke from those that had the guard of him;
    And with his mad attendant and himself,
    Each one with ireful passion, with drawn swords,
    Met us again, and, madly bent on us,
    Chased us away; till, raising of more aid,
    We came again to bind them. Then they fled
    Into this abbey, whither we pursued them;
    And here the abbess shuts the gates on us,
    And will not suffer us to fetch him out,
    Nor send him forth, that we may bear him hence.   165   160
    Therefore, most gracious Duke, with thy command
    Let him be brought forth, and borne hence for help.
DUKE.   Long since thy husband served me in my wars;
    And I to thee engaged a prince's word,
    When thou didst make him master of thy bed,
    To do him all the grace and good I could.
    Go, some of you, knock at the abbey-gate,
    And bid the lady abbess come to me.
    I will determine this before I stir.

Enter a Servant

SERV.   O mistress, mistress, shift and save yourself!   170
    My master and his man are both broke loose,
    Beaten the maids a-row, and bound the doctor,

148 *take order for*] take measures for settling, or dealing with.
150 *strong escape*] escape effected by strength.

Whose beard they have singed off with brands of fire;
And ever, as it blazed, they threw on him
Great pails of puddled mire to quench the hair:
My master preaches patience to him, and the while
His man with scissors nicks him like a fool;
And sure, unless you send some present help,
Between them they will kill the conjurer.

ADR.   Peace, fool! thy master and his man are here;   180
And that is false thou dost report to us.

SERV.   Mistress, upon my life, I tell you true;
I have not breathed almost since I did see it.
He cries for you, and vows, if he can take you,
To scorch your face and to disfigure you.

[*Cry within.*

Hark, hark! I hear him, mistress: fly, be gone!

DUKE.   Come, stand by me; fear nothing. Guard with halberds!

ADR.   Ay me, it is my husband! Witness you,
That he is borne about invisible:
Even now we housed him in the abbey here;   190
And now he's there, past thought of human reason.

Enter ANTIPHOLUS *of Ephesus and* DROMIO *of Ephesus*

ANT. E.   Justice, most gracious Duke, O, grant me justice!
Even for the service that long since I did thee,
When I bestrid thee in the wars, and took
Deep scars to save thy life; even for the blood
That then I lost for thee, now grant me justice.

ÆGE.   Unless the fear of death doth make me dote,
I see my son Antipholus, and Dromio.

ANT. E.   Justice, sweet prince, against that woman there!
She whom thou gavest to me to be my wife,   200
That hath abused and dishonour'd me
Even in the strength and height of injury:
Beyond imagination is the wrong
That she this day hath shameless thrown on me.

DUKE.   Discover how, and thou shalt find me just.

ANT. E.   This day, great Duke, she shut the doors upon me,
While she with harlots feasted in my house.

177 *nicks*] clips or crops close. It seems to have been the customary way in which fools'
hair was cut.
194 *bestrid*] stood over thee when fallen, protected thee.
207 *harlots*] a common term of reproach often applied to rascally men as well as to wan-
ton women.

DUKE. A grievous fault! Say, woman, didst thou so?
ADR. No, my good lord: myself, he and my sister
    To-day did dine together. So befal my soul   210
    As this is false he burthens me withal!
LUC. Ne'er may I look on day, nor sleep on night,
    But she tells to your Highness simple truth!
ANG. O perjured woman! They are both forsworn:
    In this the madman justly chargeth them.
ANT. E. My liege, I am advised what I say;
    Neither disturbed with the effect of wine,
    Nor heady-rash, provoked with raging ire,
    Albeit my wrongs might make one wiser mad.
    This woman lock'd me out this day from dinner: 220
    That goldsmith there, were he not pack'd with her,
    Could witness it, for he was with me then;
    Who parted with me to go fetch a chain,
    Promising to bring it to the Porpentine,
    Where Balthazar and I did dine together.
    Our dinner done, and he not coming thither,
    I went to seek him: in the street I met him,
    And in his company that gentleman.
    There did this perjured goldsmith swear me down
    That I this day of him received the chain,   230
    Which, God he knows, I saw not: for the which
    He did arrest me with an officer.
    I did obey; and sent my peasant home
    For certain ducats: he with none return'd.
    Then fairly I bespoke the officer
    To go in person with me to my house.
    By the way we met my wife, her sister, and a rabble more
    Of vile confederates. Along with them
    They brought one Pinch, a hungry lean-faced villain,
    A mere anatomy, a mountebank,   240
    A threadbare juggler, and a fortune-teller,
    A needy, hollow-eyed, sharp-looking wretch,
    A living dead man: this pernicious slave,
    Forsooth, took on him as a conjurer;
    And, gazing in mine eyes, feeling my pulse,
    And with no face, as 't were, outfacing me,
    Cries out, I was possess'd. Then all together
    They fell upon me, bound me, bore me thence,
    And in a dark and dankish vault at home

---

248 *They fell upon me*] The ordinary contemporary method of dealing with lunatics.

There left me and my man, both bound together;   250
Till, gnawing with my teeth my bonds in sunder,
I gain'd my freedom, and immediately
Ran hither to your Grace; whom I beseech
To give me ample satisfaction
For these deep shames and great indignities.

ANG.   My lord, in truth, thus far I witness with him,
    That he dined not at home, but was lock'd out.

DUKE.   But had he such a chain of thee or no?

ANG.   He had, my lord: and when he ran in here,
    These people saw the chain about his neck.   260

SEC. MER.   Besides, I will be sworn these ears of mine
    Heard you confess you had the chain of him,
    After you first forswore it on the mart:
    And thereupon I drew my sword on you;
    And then you fled into this abbey here,
    From whence, I think, you are come by miracle.

ANT. E.   I never came within these abbey-walls;
    Nor ever didst thou draw thy sword on me:
    I never saw the chain, so help me Heaven!
    And this is false you burthen me withal.   270

DUKE.   Why, what an intricate impeach is this!
    I think you all have drunk of Circe's cup.
    If here you housed him, here he would have been;
    If he were mad, he would not plead so coldly:
    You say he dined at home; the goldsmith here
    Denies that saying. Sirrah, what say you?

DRO. E.   Sir, he dined with her there, at the Porpentine.

COUR.   He did; and from my finger snatch'd that ring.

ANT. E.   'T is true, my liege; this ring I had of her.

DUKE.   Saw'st thou him enter at the abbey here?   280

COUR.   As sure, my liege, as I do see your Grace.

DUKE.   Why, this is strange. Go call the abbess hither.
    I think you are all mated, or stark mad.

                    [*Exit one to the* Abbess.

ÆGE.   Most mighty Duke, vouchsafe me speak a word:
    Haply I see a friend will save my life,
    And pay the sum that may deliver me.

DUKE.   Speak freely, Syracusian, what thou wilt.

ÆGE.   Is not your name, sir, call'd Antipholus?
    And is not that your bondman, Dromio?

DRO. E.   Within this hour I was his bondman, sir,   290

283 *mated*] See note on III, ii, 54, *supra*.

, I thank him, gnaw'd in two my cords:
　　m I Dromio, and his man unbound.
　　m sure you both of you remember me.

DRO. E.　Ourselves we do remember, sir, by you;
　　For lately we were bound, as you are now.
　　You are not Pinch's patient, are you, sir?

ÆGE.　Why look you strange on me? you know me well.

ANT. E.　I never saw you in my life till now.

ÆGE.　O, grief hath changed me since you saw me last,
　　And careful hours with time's deformed hand　　　　300
　　Have written strange defeatures in my face:
　　But tell me yet, dost thou not know my voice?

ANT. E.　Neither.

ÆGE.　Dromio, nor thou?

DRO. E.　　　　　　　　　No, trust me, sir, nor I.

ÆGE.　I am sure thou dost.

DRO. E.　Ay, sir, but I am sure I do not; and whatsoever a man
　　denies, you are now bound to believe him.

ÆGE.　Not know my voice! O time's extremity,
　　Hast thou so crack'd and splitted my poor tongue　　310
　　In seven short years, that here my only son
　　Knows not my feeble key of untuned cares?
　　Though now this grained face of mine be hid
　　In sap-consuming winter's drizzled snow,
　　And all the conduits of my blood froze up,
　　Yet hath my night of life some memory,
　　My wasting lamps some fading glimmer left,
　　My dull deaf ears a little use to hear:
　　All these old witnesses—I cannot err—
　　Tell me thou art my son Antipholus.　　　　320

ANT. E.　I never saw my father in my life.

ÆGE.　But seven years since, in Syracusa, boy,
　　Thou know'st we parted: but perhaps, my son,
　　Thou shamest to acknowledge me in misery.

ANT. E.　The Duke and all that know me in the city
　　Can witness with me that it is not so:
　　I ne'er saw Syracusa in my life.

DUKE.　I tell thee, Syracusian, twenty years

300 *careful hours*] hours full of care, anxiety, sorrow.
301 *defeatures*] See note on II, i, 98, *supra*.
312 *my feeble key, etc.*] my weak and discordant tone of voice which is caused by my
　　griefs.
313 *grained*] furrowed like the grain of wood.

Have I been patron to Antipholus,
During which time he ne'er saw Syracusa: 330
I see thy age and dangers make thee dote.

Re-enter Abbess, *with* ANTIPHOLUS of Syracuse *and* DROMIO of
    Syracuse

ABB.   Most mighty Duke, behold a man much wrong'd.
                           [*All gather to see them.*
ADR.   I see two husbands, or mine eyes deceive me.
DUKE.   One of these men is Genius to the other;
And so of these. Which is the natural man,
And which the spirit? who deciphers them?
DRO. S.   I, sir, am Dromio: command him away.
DRO. E.   I, sir, am Dromio; pray, let me stay.
ANT. S.   Ægeon art thou not? or else his ghost?
DRO. S.   O, my old master! who hath bound him here?   340
ABB.   Whoever bound him, I will loose his bonds,
And gain a husband by his liberty.
Speak, old Ægeon, if thou be'st the man
That hadst a wife once call'd Æmilia,
That bore thee at a burthen two fair sons:
O, if thou be'st the same Ægeon, speak,
And speak unto the same Æmilia!
ÆGE.   If I dream not, thou art Æmilia:
If thou art she, tell me, where is that son
That floated with thee on the fatal raft?   350
ABB.   By men of Epidamnum he and I
And the twin Dromio, all were taken up;
But by and by rude fishermen of Corinth
By force took Dromio and my son from them,
And me they left with those of Epidamnum.
What then became of them I cannot tell;
I to this fortune that you see me in.
DUKE.   Why, here begins his morning story right:
These two Antipholuses, these two so like,
And these two Dromios, one in semblance, —   360
Besides her urging of her wreck at sea, —
These are the parents to these children,
Which accidentally are met together.
Antipholus, thou camest from Corinth first?

---

334 *Genius*] guardian angel or spirit.
358–363 *Why, here begins, etc.*] This speech of the Duke in the Folio editions is wrongly
    placed before Ægeon's speech (line 348). Capell made the necessary transposition.

ANT. S.   No, sir, not I; I came from Syracuse.

DUKE.   Stay, stand apart; I know not which is which.

ANT. E.   I came from Corinth, my most gracious lord,—

DRO. E.   And I with him.

ANT. E.   Brought to this town by that most famous warrior,
Duke Menaphon, your most renowned uncle.   370

ADR.   Which of you two did dine with me to-day?

ANT. S.   I, gentle mistress.

ADR.   And are not you my husband?

ANT. E.   No; I say nay to that.

ANT. S.   And so do I; yet did she call me so:
And this fair gentlewoman, her sister here,
Did call me brother. [*To* LUCIANA] What I told you then,
I hope I shall have leisure to make good;
If this be not a dream I see and hear.

ANG.   That is the chain, sir, which you had of me.   380

ANT. S.   I think it be, sir; I deny it not.

ANT. E.   And you, sir, for this chain arrested me.

ANG.   I think I did, sir; I deny it not.

ADR.   I sent you money, sir, to be your bail,
By Dromio; but I think he brought it not.

DRO. E.   No, none by me.

ANT. S.   This purse of ducats I received from you,
And Dromio my man did bring them me.
I see we still did meet each other's man;
And I was ta'en for him, and he for me;   390
And thereupon these ERRORS are arose.

ANT. E.   These ducats pawn I for my father here.

DUKE.   It shall not need; thy father hath his life.

COUR.   Sir, I must have that diamond from you.

ANT. E.   There, take it; and much thanks for my good cheer.

ABB.   Renowned Duke, vouchsafe to take the pains
To go with us into the abbey here,
And hear at large discoursed all our fortunes:
And all that are assembled in this place,
That by this sympathized one day's error   400
Have suffer'd wrong, go keep us company,
And we shall make full satisfaction.
Thirty-three years have I but gone in travail
Of you, my sons; and till this present hour
My heavy burthen ne'er delivered.
The Duke, my husband, and my children both,
And you the calendars of their nativity,

Go to a gossips' feast, and go with me;
After so long grief, such nativity!
DUKE.   With all my heart, I'll gossip at this feast.   410
          [*Exeunt all but* ANT. S., ANT. E., DRO. S., *and* DRO. E.
DRO. S.   Master, shall I fetch your stuff from shipboard?
ANT. E.   Dromio, what stuff of mine hast thou embark'd?
DRO. S.   Your goods that lay at host, sir, in the Centaur.
ANT. S.   He speaks to me. I am your master, Dromio:
          Come, go with us; we'll look to that anon:
          Embrace thy brother there; rejoice with him.
                              [*Exeunt* ANT. S. *and* ANT. E.
DRO. S.   There is a fat friend at your master's house,
          That kitchen'd me for you to-day at dinner:
          She now shall be my sister, not my wife.
DRO. E.   Methinks you are my glass, and not my brother: 420
          I see by you I am a sweet-faced youth.
          Will you walk in to see their gossiping?
DRO. S.   Not I, sir; you are my elder.
DRO. E.   That's a question: how shall we try it?
DRO. S.   We'll draw cuts for the senior: till then lead thou first.
DRO. E.   Nay, then, thus:
          We came into the world like brother and brother;
          And now let's go hand in hand, not one before another.
                                                  [*Exeunt.*

408, 410 *gossips' feast*] feast given to the sponsors at a christening.
409 *such nativity*] Thus the old reading. Hanmer substituted *felicity* and later editors *fes-
      tivity*, in the belief that "nativity" was a printer's repetition, through an error of vi-
      sion, of "nativity," the last word of line 407. But "nativity" harmonises somewhat
      better with the twice repeated reference to "gossips," *i.e.* sponsors at a christening.
411–412 *stuff*] See note on IV, iv, 155, *supra.*
413 *lay at host*] were lodged or stored.

PLAYS

THE ORESTEIA TRILOGY: Agamemnon, the Libation-Bearers and the Furies, Aeschylus. (0-486-29242-8)

EVERYMAN, Anonymous. (0-486-28726-2)

THE BIRDS, Aristophanes. (0-486-40886-8)

LYSISTRATA, Aristophanes. (0-486-28225-2)

THE CHERRY ORCHARD, Anton Chekhov. (0-486-26682-6)

THE SEA GULL, Anton Chekhov. (0-486-40656-3)

MEDEA, Euripides. (0-486-27548-5)

FAUST, PART ONE, Johann Wolfgang von Goethe. (0-486-28046-2)

THE INSPECTOR GENERAL, Nikolai Gogol. (0-486-28500-6)

SHE STOOPS TO CONQUER, Oliver Goldsmith. (0-486-26867-5)

GHOSTS, Henrik Ibsen. (0-486-29852-3)

A DOLL'S HOUSE, Henrik Ibsen. (0-486-27062-9)

HEDDA GABLER, Henrik Ibsen. (0-486-26469-6)

DR. FAUSTUS, Christopher Marlowe. (0-486-28208-2)

TARTUFFE, Molière. (0-486-41117-6)

BEYOND THE HORIZON, Eugene O'Neill. (0-486-29085-9)

THE EMPEROR JONES, Eugene O'Neill. (0-486-29268-1)

CYRANO DE BERGERAC, Edmond Rostand. (0-486-41119-2)

MEASURE FOR MEASURE: Unabridged, William Shakespeare. (0-486-40889-2)

FOUR GREAT TRAGEDIES: Hamlet, Macbeth, Othello, and Romeo and Juliet, William Shakespeare. (0-486-44083-4)

THE COMEDY OF ERRORS, William Shakespeare. (0-486-42461-8)

HENRY V, William Shakespeare. (0-486-42887-7)

MUCH ADO ABOUT NOTHING, William Shakespeare. (0-486-28272-4)

FIVE GREAT COMEDIES: Much Ado About Nothing, Twelfth Night, A Midsummer Night's Dream, As You Like It and The Merry Wives of Windsor, William Shakespeare. (0-486-44086-9)

OTHELLO, William Shakespeare. (0-486-29097-2)

AS YOU LIKE IT, William Shakespeare. (0-486-40432-3)

ROMEO AND JULIET, William Shakespeare. (0-486-27557-4)

A MIDSUMMER NIGHT'S DREAM, William Shakespeare. (0-486-27067-X)

THE MERCHANT OF VENICE, William Shakespeare. (0-486-28492-1)

HAMLET, William Shakespeare. (0-486-27278-8)

RICHARD III, William Shakespeare. (0-486-28747-5)